Animal Alphabed

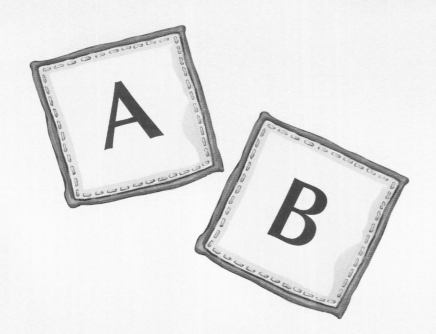

Animal Alphabed

by Margriet Ruurs

Illustrated by Jennifer Emery

WORDSONG

Boyds Mills Press

Published by Wordsong
Boyds Mills Press, Inc.
A Highlights Company
815 Church Street
Honesdale, Pennsylvania 18431
Printed in China

Library of Congress Cataloging-in-Publication Data

Ruurs, Margriet.
  Animal alphabed / by Margriet Ruurs ; illustrated by Jennifer Emery.—1st ed.
    p. cm.
  ISBN 1-59078-200-3 (alk. paper)
1. Animals—Juvenile poetry. 2. Children's poetry, Canadian. 3. Alphabet rhymes.
I. Emery, Jennifer. II. Title.

  PR9199.3.R86A84 2005
  811'.54—dc22

2004029066

First edition, 2005
The text of this book is set in 14-point Stone Serif.
The illustrations are done in watercolor.

10 9 8 7 6 5 4 3 2 1

To Barb May, who loves books.
Thank you to my editor, Wendy Murray
—M. R.

To my favorite animals: Blackie, Fezz, Nubs, and George.
—J. E.

As I fall asleep each night,
all my animals are around me.
Alligator, Armadillo, Alley Cat . . .
Cuddly creatures, from A to Z,
tucked into my animal alphabed.

Sweet dreams,
just follow the moonbeams!

Brown Bear, Badger,
bashful Bulldog
bundle up beside me.
Mama tucks us in,
quilt up to my chin.

"Good-night, sleep tight!
Don't let the bedbug bullies bite!"

But before I close my eyes, I realize . . .

B

I see Cat and Chickadee,
Camel and chubby Chipmunk,
I check my animals from A to Z,
but there's one that I don't see!
Who's not here? Who could it be?

I check each square —
one of them is just not there!

Donkey and downy Duck
tucked tightly in a hug,
drowsily I drift off to dream
of dancing dragonflies
in dainty dandelion fields.
I spent the day dreaming,

but now I have to keep sleep away
to find my animal that's gone astray!

E

Excitedly I sit up in bed,
shaking sleep from my head.
"Everybody! Perk up your ears!"
I exclaim as Elephant appears
and starts packing his trunk.

I grab Alligator, Bear, Cat, even Skunk.
Then we eagerly embark
on a rescue mission in the dark!

Flamingos float by on feathery clouds,
"Come, let's fly off
into the flamboyant sky
to find your furry or feathered friend!"
they sing as they go by.

F

Geese glide on gigantic wings.
Giraffe grins and giggles hello.
Gorilla wants a kiss,
but he's not the one I miss!

G

Here are Horse, Hamster, and Hound!
Hopping off my cloud,
I see a hundred hairy caterpillars
doing handstands on a limb.

They holler, "Hi! We're doing midnight gym!"
     "Well, hurry up and help," I say,
     "to find my friend who's run away."

H

I drop
with a plop,
open my eyes,
what a surprise!
Iguanas and ibises dance a ballet!
But, hey!

I check *again*.
A - B - C
Who is *hiding behind a tree?*

Jack Rabbit jumps into sight.
"I thought you just might join us tonight,"
he jests with a jubilant smile.
"I do hope you'll stay for a while!"
His tummy jiggles like Jell-O.
He is such a jolly fellow,
giving me juicy jelly beans, purple and yellow.

I remember to count my animals,
check each square.
Better start looking everywhere!

J

I climb on Kangaroo's back,
quickly he carries me into the jungle,
where Komodo dragons in kilts and kimonos
kick up their heels,
and cuddly koalas play kazoos.

Kangaroo knows I'm feeling blue.
"We'll find him," he coos
with a kind little smile.
"It just might take a while."

A Little bit later, I lazily yawn,
laboring to stay awake.
We lumber and lie on a lawn.
A lovely ladybug brings us
a luscious lollipop cake.
Licking my fingers,
I curl up for a little catnap
on a lovable, large lion's lap.

L

I wake to a **M**argarine moon
and hear a mystical, magical tune
sung by a million magpies
as they float through the midnight skies.

My missing friend —
Is he black and white, too?
I cannot find him. Can you?

M

Nine nightingales nudge each other and sing in unison, "He's not in the forest, nor in the meadows."
A grumpy night owl in her nightie peeks from her nest.
"Hush your singing; I need my rest!"

O

"Oh no, oh dear, I overslept!"
groans the old owl.
"I am afraid I didn't hear
any of the coyotes howl!
And no, my dear, I sadly fear
I did not see your friend.

But since you seek, why don't you peek
behind the old maple tree,
You never know what you might see!"

Puffing, Panda putters by,
and, panting, he pleads,
"Please come to our picnic!"

P

A party specifically for you!
Promise to bring your friends, too.
It's at the Purple Palace in the park.
We hope you will partake
of the plum pudding, pastries and cake,
pancakes and pizza, purple pineapple stew.
We'll have cream puffs and pretzels
and party hats, too.
And pomegranate punch to wash down
this whole perfect lunch!"

Queen Petunia

The **Q**ueen is our host
as we feast on great quantities of kumquat toast.
I quietly watch some quarreling quackers
devour all of the cucumber crackers
as they quibble and quip
over who gets the most.

Then I quiz the queen
to see if she's seen
my friend who is so long gone.
She gazes out over the lawn
and questions, "Is he white, orange, yellow, or black?"
"I don't know!" I quiver, "I just want him back!"

Where is he? Will I find him at last?
Let's quickly resume our friend-finding quest!

Q

Roaming across the royal palace grounds.
I see ravenous rabbits eat red raspberries 'til their bellies are round.
We watch a reindeer race that never seems to end.
Ravens ask riddles but don't know the answers.
I have to go and see what my chance is
to rescue my rambunctious, runaway friend!

Some seventy-seven sheep send me off to sleep.
As I slumber, it silently starts to snow.
Six silly scarecrows squeal and throw
snowballs at my nose,
startling me wide awake!
I shiver and shake
off the snow.

Well, what do you know?
Do you think that he might
be hiding in all of this white?

S

Ten turtles in turquoise tracksuits
team up with toucans
to tackle the task of finding my friend.
One of them tells me he's spotted the tiniest tip of a tail!
But I'm too tired; it's to no avail.

Unicorn ushers us into the palace hall.
Under an umbrella is a table full of treats.
She pours tea for us all, from a silver urn
and serves us sweets.
When it is my turn,
I choose with utmost care
the most scrumptious upside-down cupcake there!

U

In the Vaulted vestibule, the queen sings
virtuous verses by the vibrating strings
of a violin.
Sipping my tea, I begin to grin,
for behind a violet veil,
I spot stripes and — is that a tail?!

V

A great **W**hite whale,
looking a little bit pale,
winks at me, then whacks her tail.
"I wonder," she whispers with a smile,
"if you will find your wandering friend in a while?"

An eXtremely extroverted ox
accompanies the Queen on xylophone.
We dance off our socks
'til it's time to go home.

Once more I count animals,
check each square.
The missing one still isn't there!

Y

Oh, how I **Y**earn to lie in bed
as sleepy dreams dance through my head.
I yawn once more.
A yellow moon tells me that soon
I'll find what I've been yearning for.

I toss and turn, rub my eyes.
Zigging, I zoom back through the skies
and land in my own cozy bed!
I sit up straight, shake my head.

Quickly, check each square.

Are all of my animals there?

Alligator, Bear, and Cat
safely tucked in my animal alphabed.
Giraffe, Jackrabbit, Kangaroo,
Lion, Magpie, Owl, and Panda, too.
Sheep, Turtle, Whale, and . . . what is that?
Who has fallen on the floor?!
It's ZEBRA I couldn't find before!
Lots of hugging, lots of kissing,
It was Zebra that was missing!
Count his ears, kiss his nose, tug his tail,
check his stripes of white and black.
I am so glad I found him back!

Now sleep, my little friend,
hold on tightly to my hand,
follow your dreams
all through the night,
'til the morning skies turn bright.